The story so far...

Mysti, having discovered that she's half human, is still coming to come to terms with the implications, like being able to tell the odd lie and feeling grumpy when things don't go to plan. It's very confusing for Ella who is used to having Mysti around to help her out. Now she has to cope with Mysti getting into scrapes as well.

Ravva, you have been a loyal servant to the Drow and now your time has come. You have an important mission. Hidden folk are fools: they waste their powers helping humans. They must be stopped and taught the error of their ways. My own son was sent to do this, but he has failed me.

You are to find him and bring him to me.

I understand.

The daughter of the Goldress, Mysti, is friend to a human girl. I want you to wreak havoc in her life so she denounces the hidden folk and their meddling ways.

It will be an honour.

2

3

5

7

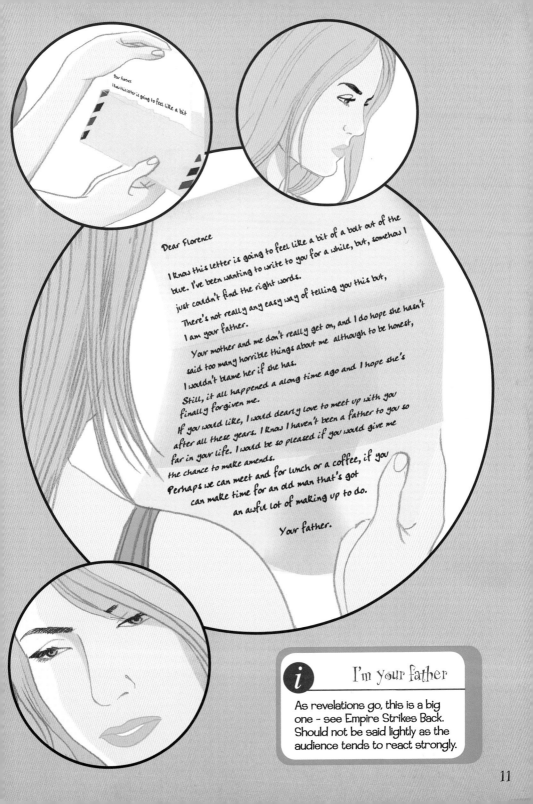

Dear Florence

I know this letter is going to feel like a bit of a bolt out of the blue. I've been wanting to write to you for a while, but, somehow I just couldn't find the right words.

There's not really any easy way of telling you this but, I am your father.

Your mother and me don't really get on, and I do hope she hasn't said too many horrible things about me although to be honest, I wouldn't blame her if she has.

Still, it all happened a along time ago and I hope she's finally forgiven me.

If you would like, I would dearly love to meet up with you after all these years. I know I haven't been a father to you so far in your life. I would be so pleased if you would give me the chance to make amends.

Perhaps we can meet and for lunch or a coffee, if you can make time for an old man that's got an awful lot of making up to do.

Your father.

> **ⓘ   I'm your father**
>
> As revelations go, this is a big one - see Empire Strikes Back. Should not be said lightly as the audience tends to react strongly.

11

12

13

15

Fairyland...

18

19

20

21

23

25

Fairyland...

29

Abby's bedroom...

Let's face it, I have no idea what it feels like, so you're going to have to tell me. What was it like?

What was what like?

The boyfriend stuff. You know, being in love...

Well, you have to realise it was some time ago...

Just get on with it. It's the best we've got.

OK. Well it was wonderful: my heart was pounding, but I didn't want to give anything away...

Heart pounding. Go on...

I felt sort of wobbly, you know, when I looked at him and when I spoke my voice sort of quavered a bit.

35

39

40

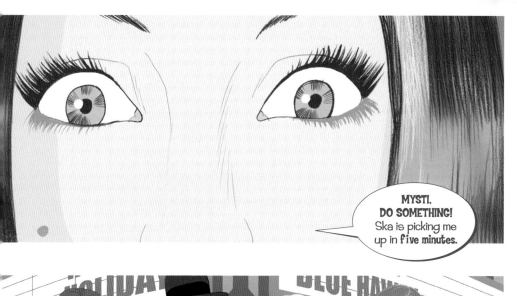

41

43

45

51

55

61

63

'ello 'ello 'ello. Thought you said you'd mysteriously vanish back to that kingdom of yours, but surprise, surprise, here you still are.

My father will be vengeful when he hears you have imprisoned his son Ska'lath with bars of iron.

And the judge is going to be pretty vengeful when they hear you were driving at 100 miles an hour in a stolen car, or will you be escaping from the court as well?

You will not laugh when my father's kingdom takes over the earth.

You're right. It's not a rib tickler, is it? Let's get you interviewed, then you can get back to whatever planet it is you live on, Sonny Jim.

66

71

You're not going to the Vent?

It's not a big deal...

Ella! It won't be the same without you.

Don't suppose you'll even notice.

Valentine's day...

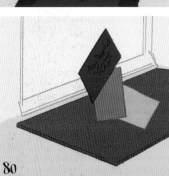

82

85

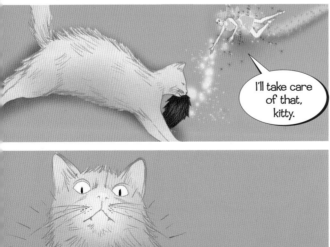

89

91

92

93

The Valentine's Vent...

EXIT

Valentine Love

94

Valentine's Vent

Fairyland...

Valentine's Vent...

100

101

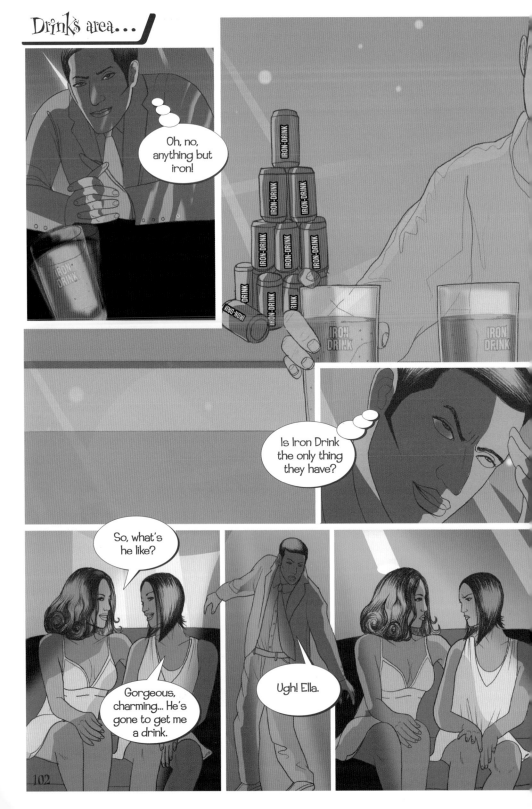

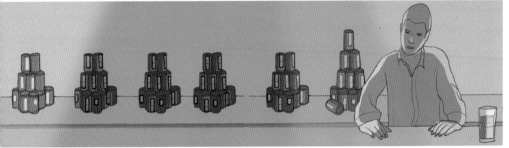

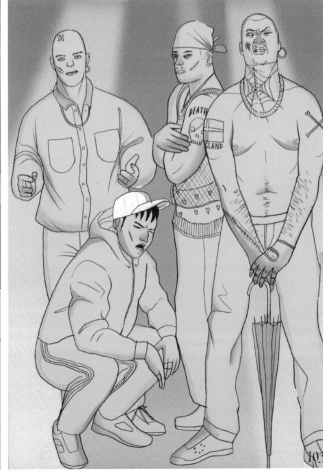

107

OK, if you say so, but it looks like you've got enough problems...

Ah... that's better. The pollen count must be high and I have a terrible nut allergy.

We don't want that kind of behaviour in here, so why don't you apologise to the ladies and explain that you will be buying them new drinks. Then you can go and ask at the bar if they have a mop and bucket you can clean up with.

Right.

But it weren't my fault.

Wow!

Wasn't your fault, moron. And yes it was. Next time be more careful. You can't go round like a clumsy oaf knocking things over.

In Episode 6...

Ella's on a French Exchange in the City of Lights: Paris! The glamour of the Champs Elysées, the Latin Quarter and... a pig farm? Zut alors!

But will Mysti's magic work in France and will she and Ella manage to evade Rav, the suave undercover Drow?

All my adventures are now available to buy from my website
www.mysti.co.uk/shop